Smokin'

We were all pretty shocked at Ernie. I mean, we all knew him from last year before he had been a Spaz, and he had been at least capable of the fundamentals—he had never shown this kind of giggly incompetence before. I mean, he was acting as if he just didn't give a crap out there, but none of us wanted to believe that because we kind of liked him. Yet there was no doubt about his screwing up, and when he turned to the coach with red eyes and a very out-of-place smile that said, "Jeez, sorry, but what's the big deal? I'm just a Spaz anyway," I think we all felt a chill go through us. We knew something was wrong with Ernie, and I think we all knew what it was.

WOODSIE, AGAIN

WOODSIE, AGAIN

BRUCE BROOKS

A LAURA GERINGER BOOK

HarperTrophy®
A Division of HarperCollinsPublishers

Woodsie, Again
Copyright © 1999 by Bruce Brooks

Library of Congress Cataloging-in-Publication Data
Brooks, Bruce.
  Woodsie, again / by Bruce Brooks.
      p.   cm. — (The Wolfbay Wings ; #12)
  "A Laura Geringer book."
  Summary: As the Wolfbay Wings make their way into the
play-offs, several team members seem to be using marijuana
to deal with the pressure and the whole team suffers because
of it.
  ISBN 0-06-440729-2 (pbk.) — ISBN 0-06-028058-1 (lib. bdg.)
  [1. Hockey—Fiction. 2. Marijuana—Fiction. 3. Drug
abuse—Fiction.] I. Title. II. Series: Brooks, Bruce.
Wolfbay Wings ; #12.
PZ7.B7913Wr   1999   98-54997
[Fic]—DC21   CIP
                                                     AC

Typography by Steve Scott
1   2   3   4   5   6   7   8   9   10
❖
First Edition
Visit us on the World Wide Web!
http://www.harperchildrens.com

WOODSIE, AGAIN

Well, in two years I have played a lot of hockey and learned a lot of hockey too, which would figure. I mean, you would have to be some kind of dope to play with the quality players I've had the chance to play with, under the kind of coaching I've received, and not come out of it all quite a bit further on than where you were when you started.

Last season, I played Squirt A's for the Wolfbay Wings, which the year before had been the total champs of everything except the entire U.S., where they finished second. Then their best players jumped to another club, and they had to pick up scrubs like me to fill their jerseys and they lost a *whole* lot of games, mostly because of us scrubs. But somehow we loved it—we had a great time.

My mother, who is a Winner, came to our first home game and watched us lose 13–0, then skipped the rest of the season. But my dad became a scrubby assistant coach and skated with us almost every practice even though he was a lousy skater and the players often had to help him up off the ice. But they liked him. Sometimes he spent games behind us on the bench, handing out water bottles to shifts that had just come off the ice, as the team went down in flames once more. Hey, those squeeze-bottles and stuff are important—when you're going down in flames but you need to feel like an athlete about it, the props matter.

But as I said, somehow, mostly because these are some awesome good guys and the coach is an honest man and hockey is a great game, we had a strangely respectable hoot of a season.

This season we moved up an age level, becoming the Peewee A travel team. Most of last year's Peewees had moved up to Bantams, so we pretty much got to move *en masse*, as they say in French (I take French this year). There were three leftover players, one of our deserters came back for part of the season, we got a new kid, and I spent part of the year injured, but all together we managed to establish a teamwide tight-defense philosophy, of shutting every opportunity down for the bad guys, and making the most of our own. We played very alert hockey, scored key goals when we needed them, and won a lot of games, most of them close.

I can barely describe the difference between a game last year and one this year. Last year, there was nothing at stake in any game—from the start of the year we were the dogs of the league, the joke team. And by the time we began to show some pride and some hockey sense near the end of the season it was too late to make any difference in the standings anyhow.

But the pride had put us on the right track, and it carried over. This year, first or second place was always on the line, for every game, every *play*; man, it was tight out there, but like nothing else in the world can be but hockey, it was *tight* and *wild*. Because you never know what kind of a bounce that puck will take, no matter how much you think you're in control.

So, okay, first difference, the games mattered. Second difference, the players bore down. We stayed loose in the locker room, but when we were on the ice we were as tough about our jobs as if you were trying to take food away from our families. Believe it or not, this all added up to more fun. We looked grim but we were enjoying ourselves more, because we knew what we were doing.

Then, there was the matter of respect, first from ourselves, and later from the other teams. Some of those bozos didn't get around to catching on that we were no longer the wipes we were the year before until the last couple of weeks of this season, when they finally realized that the "Wolfbay" team ahead of them in the standings was us, and we were about to pound their tails into submission in a 2–1 Wolfbay victory.

This year, we were granted the right to "check" the whole year, and some of our guys went to summer clinics on checking, you could tell. But more important than that, some of our guys got woken up by last year's half-season of hitting, and realized that they *loved* the physical part of the game.

I was one of them.

I loved every part of the hitting—the little digs in close when you were fighting for a puck in your skates in the corner, the whoa! highlight-film hip-checks in open ice, the aggressive forecheck-pinning of a defenseman against the boards behind the net, holding him there while the puck got ahead of his stick and one of your teammates snapped a surprise shot on the goalie—I loved all of it.

My injury, a cheap poke in the breadbasket by a teammate, laid me low early in the season, but because what he had done scared him into good sense, he became a very valuable guy. For me, the injury did not have the expected result: Instead of making me more wary, it made me more aggressive. I was determined to come back earlier than my doctors predicted, and I did, and I came back a better, harder hockey player. Then our team's best defenseman, Barry, who has always moved among us in silence, surprised me one day by offering to teach me a lot of the tricks of the trade, and I made the most of it. He was a great teacher—quick, clear, ready to move on to the next thing once he felt I had gotten the piece of the game we were working on, leaving it to me to practice and refine what I had learned.

So, how could I not get better?

Our new style with our new people playing their best worked so well that we won the titles in both of our leagues, and qualified in a high spot for the play-offs.

The old Wings knew all about the play-offs. Here are some of their comments:

Dooby: "None of the teams we play will suck. So we can't lose our focus or our sense of danger for the whole game."

Cody: "It's, like, so intense out there you can get a headache."

Prince: "We can beat everybody, if we concentrate."

Boot: "The Boot will just play hockey."

Nathan, our captain, who has never been in play-offs: "I'm too nervous to talk about it."

Zip, our goalie: "There is no difference at all in the play-offs. It's still a bunch of weenie jerks whacking their stupid shots at me. Same puck, right? Same sticks, same skates, same ice. All this 'Ooooh, it's the *play-offs!*' crap is just you guys preparing an excuse if you lose."

You can always count on Zip to zero in on it all.

two

After one practice between the end of the season and the start of the mysterious play-offs—we still didn't know which team we would be playing in the draw—Coach Cooper gave us a little lecture in the locker room.

"I want to talk about our team more than about the nature of games in the play-offs," he said. "Your teammates who have been there can tell you about that stuff better than I can. The obvious point, which I'm sure you've thought about already, is to expect high-quality intensity from our competition for the whole game, and to stick to our style with full alertness and cool intelligence no matter what kinds of different styles we face, some of which may be surprising. We are good enough to force them to adjust to us, ultimately—we needn't try to change our game to adjust to them."

He paused, and cleared his throat. "Now, I want

to talk about our team. Or it might be more accurate to say, I want to *ask* you something about our team."

"The answer is, Veuve-Clicquot," said Zip. "We find the bouquet of Bollinger's to be rather pretentious and, though amusing, a touch on the greenish side. Either Veuve-Clicquot, or Cherry Pepsi."

"Thank you, Zip, my secretary has made careful note of your beverage choices," said the coach without losing his momentum. "What I was going to ask is this: In the regular season we have followed last year's policy of giving each line, including what you people so proudly call 'the Spaz Line—'"

Here the four or five players thus referred to because of their generally inferior skills banged their sticks on the floor and whooped it up.

"Thank you for showing your pride," said the coach, "and let's see what kind of pride it is. My question: For the play-offs, given the higher quality of the competition's play and the unrelenting intensity we will face, does the team wish to change our policy and adopt one that will allow me to occasionally substitute a higher line for a Spaz Line's shift to put on the ice our more skilled players, or certain players better suited, say, to cover another team's particular threat, even if it means that other players lose some ice time? Don't get me wrong. I like our equality as it is, so I will be happy to stick with it. At the same time, I'd be a liar if I said I thought it wouldn't be a liability in the play-offs. It's up to you guys."

"You can tell from your son's behavior that you are one of those permissive people who just won't take responsibility and make a firm decision," said Zip. "Pass the buck. I bet you ask Cody every morning, 'Would iddle Snookums like to go to school today, or would he prefer to stay home and play with his trucks?'"

"I'm more into Barbies," said Cody.

"Whatever."

There was a moment of silence, then I said, "I think a self-appointed Spaz ought to speak first."

A kid named Mark, whom we call Foots because he is a terrible skater who's always getting his feet tangled together and going down face-first, sometimes blocking a lot of shots, stood up and grinned at everyone.

"Not only are we willing to give up our ice time

in favor of better guys," he said, "but Coach is giving us a way to sit down in honor. Frankly, we're already chickenhearted, and scared as crap of messing up and getting the team knocked out of the play-offs." He looked around him at the other less-skilled players and said, "Right, dudes?"

Four or five voices said, "Right," and "Tell the man, Foots," and "We'll practice up on our cheering."

The coach looked around at the rest of us. "What about you?"

"Double-shift me whenever you want to, Coach," said Zip, in a mock-fervent tone. Zip, of course, already plays the entire game.

Dooby said, "Fine. Just keep in mind, more ice time means more pay."

"That's right," said Prince. "Double-shifting means double wages, or we get the union on your tail."

Boot brought it back to earth by saying, "The Boot never feels fatigue and is available for any extension of duty on the ice."

"The Boot is available for any chance to add to his gaudy goal total, you mean," said Dooby. Boot smiled, minimally. Dooby went on, "Seriously,

Coach—well, let our captain say it for us."

Nathan stood up, shrugged, and said, "You're the boss. Put us on the ice whenever you want."

"Except on my birthday," said Cody. "Then I get to play the whole game, every shift."

"When's your birthday?" I asked.

"August sixth," said Cody.

The play-offs end by April 1.

With the team in agreement, everyone went back to the usual locker room mix of loud joking, silent loosening of skate laces, tape-ball warfare, goofy stories cut off in the middle, and a song from Prince. The only thing different was that now we had a new policy. Personally, I was glad.

three

At our next practice, there were some changes from our routine. The biggest was that in the course of the drills, the coach took each of us into a corner and made us fight him for the puck. Then he put the puck back into play as soon as he won it, which was every time against everyone.

But sometimes before chipping it once more into contention, he would stop and show us exactly how he had won it the previous two or three times. Then he'd make us practice these techniques against him until we had them at least minimally down. He was very physical, and though he didn't fully use his extra hundred pounds and foot and a half of height, he often *did* use a bit of his strength beyond our own, making us battle uphill.

I came out of my corner drill sweating as hard as I usually do only by the third period of intense games. But it was worth it. I felt I could beat any other kid in the corners now, and come away with the puck, clean. Normally, I am very energetic when I battle in the corners, but I seem to be too aware that I am a defenseman. Instead of winning the puck I usually manage only to tie up the opponent's offensive player and the puck until one of my teammates snaps it away or a face-off is whistled. I never really try to *possess* it as soon as I can and turn and aggressively make something offensive start the other way.

It was an intense practice the whole way through. Everyone did even the familiar drills with an extra ferocity, finishing with shots that had more on them, and that were more carefully placed.

Zip was, of course, both pissed off that we got a few past him and scornful that we even tried.

"*Now* we discover the corners of the net," he said, after kicking out a sharp shot at the far post by Dooby. "We're in the *play-offs*, so we're *men*. Never again will we hit the goalie in the logo on his sweater, right? Every shot from now on will make him strain so that he injures a tendon and we have to go through the first round with Java in goal, or maybe Shark. Quick ol' Shark—that's the ticket. So, go ahead," he said, as his blocker deflected a rising puck from Cody, who shot to the top corner over the cross-bar, "and show that new play-off testosterone. *Zip* doesn't mind, no sir."

A couple of times, while I was waiting in line for my turn at drills and kind of gazing around the rink, I noticed something unusual. There were four or five players over by the boards, not in line for the drills at all. Although they were keeping an eye on the practice, they were also clowning around, pretending to bash each other into the boards, purposely tripping one another by hooking both skates . . . stuff like that. They were laughing much harder than their pranks seemed to call for. They always made it to the tail end of every line for drills, so they never really missed anything, but I could see their faces through their masks and they were always grinning. And I have to say their performance in the drills was pretty bad.

Of course, the fact was that this was the Spaz Line who was screwing around. I mean, they never did well in drills anyway, though they usually tried a lot harder than they were now.

One night while watching them, I looked

around to see if anyone else was noticing. Coach was in the corner doing his intense one-on-one thing, so he at least didn't see the Spazzes goofing.

The leader in the screwing around seemed to be Ernie. He was an interesting and difficult case on this team. Last year he had been a "regular player," though definitely the last member of the non-Spaz Line as far as skills and hockey sense went; he had gotten his regular shifts on the third line, just above the Spazzes, and frankly he had played worse than some of those guys more than once.

When Shark started to improve and moved off the Spaz Line last year, Ernie had been one of the players to rotate through his spot. This year, to make the travel Peewee A's, he had played on the Spaz Line all year and didn't seem to mind it. Basically, Ernie was a cheerful and placid kid, who seemed to enjoy being the best player by far on the Spaz Line.

So I wondered what this extra joking and stuff was about. Okay, Coach had said maybe the Spazzes wouldn't play as much in the play-offs, but it went without saying that they were still Wings all the way, and were expected to conduct themselves like Wings, which meant concentrating at practice and hustling all-out, with focus and seriousness. Especially because this was the play-offs.

four

We got the draw today; Coach told us at the start of practice that we would be playing Easton, a team from eastern Maryland that's always full of great skaters and scorers because it's the only hockey team for miles around, and so draws only the "best" from among the farm kids.

We often run into Easton kids at camps. They are always some of the biggest hotshots. I don't mean they play poorly. I only mean that their coach, faced with forty kids who can all skate fast and shoot hard and elude defenses all on their own, will be bound to make up his team of kids who can skate fast and shoot hard and take it over the blue line one-on-three.

This kind of team should be lunchmeat for us.

No disrespect intended. Hot dogs have great skills. But hot dogs play right into our hands. We know how to check them and frustrate them and take away the only kind of game they know how to play. They have a terrible time adjusting, because they never stop their flashy rushes to learn all the little nasty tricks, the hip bumps and skate-kicks and stick-lifts and poke-checks that turn an 8–6 shootout after which everyone says "Wow! That was fun!" into a 1–0 dogfight after which everyone says, "Did anyone score or do we have to play OT?"

If you tell me the score of a game was 8–6, I will tell you we probably lost; if you tell me it was 1–0, I'll bet my lucky laces we won.

Our practice was still ferocious and unrelenting. You don't take anything for granted in hockey. There are too many variables, too many funny bounces of the puck—chips out of the ice, or spikes sticking up from it, dead spots on the boards, unintentional screens of the goalie, mis-hit slap shots that throw off his timing and trickle in, passes that hit the tape of a stick weirdly and hop in an unexpected way. You can never count on things going smoothly as plays drawn on a chalkboard. The fact is, a hockey player is an improviser.

Tonight we spent the last half of practice *trying*

to cause such surprises, so the coach could show us different ways to adjust to them. At one point, during a two-on-two drill, he built a small hill out of ice shavings and water that froze immediately right in the path of the obvious pass the offensive players would make. But he told them to make it anyway. The puck went wild. It ski-jumped into the receiving player's shin pads, tilted onto its edge and rolled slowly behind him as he sped at the cage, hopped and tumbled end over end so he had to catch it with one hand and drop it back into his path and get his hand back onto his stick in time to shoot—lots of things.

The coach knew of a spot in the back dasher behind the cage and to the right, from which the puck would always rebound with outrageous liveliness, as if the spot were made of rubber. Time and time again he would send an offensive team in onside and fire the puck at that spot so that it bounced back past the defensemen into the path of a shocked but delighted shooter, who fired on Zip from the circle, or whipped a pass cross-ice to an open teammate if Zip had anticipated the bounce and set himself for the shot.

It was great. And at times very funny. But still, it never seemed quite as funny to the rest of us as it did to those guys from the Spaz contingent.

One day I noticed them goofing off to the side of the main practice again. It really bugged me. Ernie didn't even bother to skate over at the last minute and get into line for one of the drills—he just leaned on the boards, chuckling to himself. The other players who had been goofing with him joined the drill at the end of the line, but they kept looking back over their shoulders at him. It looked like a couple of them wished they had skipped the drill and played it cool too, like good old Ernie. He seemed to have become some sort of leader all of a sudden, but a leader of laughing at the wrong times and slacking off.

I couldn't figure it out. Ernie had always been a hard worker and a sincere player. This time, when I looked around the rink, I noticed that I wasn't the only one watching Ernie. I could swear that the coach's gaze lingered on him before he turned it back to the drills.

After the practice, Prince skated over to me. "You got eyes for our amused mates?"

"They did it last practice too," I said. "Laughed at everything."

"Unless I miss my guess, those boys have been smoking a little boo."

"Marijuana?"

He rolled his eyes. "Yes, Woodsie."

I was in a state of shock—and speechless. Finally I managed to say, "Before *hockey* practice?"

The guys in question were up ahead of us trying to stick shavings down each other's necks. "Either that or they got a bad case of the immatures all of a sudden," said Prince.

"But—"

"Well, Coach told them their responsibilities on the ice, at least during games, was likely to be reduced. Maybe they decided to go all the way and just act like spectators."

"They could influence players Coach is counting on."

"They'll influence others, all right," he said coolly.

I seized on an important fact. "But we don't actually know, do we?"

Prince shook his head. "That we don't."

I looked at him. He was watching me with a bemused look from inside his cage. "What you're really saying to me is, 'You, Woodsie, are the only one who doesn't know.' How are *you* so sure, Prince? When did you start getting so much experience with pot smokers?" I suddenly felt very naive.

He answered seriously. "My grandfather used to drive me around and point people out. 'There's a man been smoking a little something,' he'd say, or we'd be in a restaurant and he'd count his change very carefully, which he never does, and I'd ask why, and without looking up he'd say 'Our waiter's stoned.' It shocked me at first. It shocked me there were so many people smoking, but it shocked me even more that he *knew*. 'You can't work in music and avoid exposure to every kind of drug,' he said. 'I worked in music forty years.'"

"Did he—"

"First thing I asked him. He shook his head. 'Didn't drink anything with alcohol in it, either,' which I figured was true because he still doesn't. I asked him why. He looked me in the eye and asked me a question. 'Is it hard to sing beautifully, on pitch, with clever improvisations?' I said it was indeed hard. 'Does it require physical precision and mental quickness?' I said those were exactly the things most called upon. He nodded, and said those were also the things dope got rid of first. 'Drugs and alcohol are'—we were speaking French but he said . . . how would you say it in English?—'*anti-precision*'." Prince laughed. 'That is why people take them,' he said. 'People get fatigued with being precise.'"

I thought for a minute. We were almost at the gate. "Did he only talk about singing? Or did he mention your hockey playing too?"

"He didn't have to," Prince said over his shoulder as he walked toward the locker room.

In the locker room it was all I could do to keep my eyes off the four players. And I couldn't help noticing that they were late coming in to change, and they all came in as a group when they *did* arrive.

five

During our first game with Easton the players we suspected sat together at the end of the bench, acting all relaxed, finding almost everything very funny. For the first two periods the rest of us switched Easton off pretty easily. The more we frustrated them the more they took chances bringing their defensemen in, up ice. We got a lot of odd-man rushes back our way. Their goalie isn't very good. So by the start of the third we were leading 6–0. The Easton players had given up by this point, and if their coach could have waved a white towel and skipped the third period, he would have.

Our first line went out as usual to take the opening face-off, but the coach called them back. Then he looked down the bench and called for the Spazzes.

Their laughter ceased. "Us?" said Ernie, the defenseman and Spaz leader.

"Go out and, like, *play*?" said his left wing, looking incredulous.

"Isn't that what you put on ice skates and brightly colored sweaters and took ahold of those funny-looking sticks for?" said Coach.

"Well," said Ernie, "yeah, but, you said—"

"Need to face it off, Coach," said the ref. Easton was all set in position.

"If those guys are ready to play when they're down by six goals, I think we owe them some hockey," said Coach, his voice a little low and menacing. "Get out there *now*."

The four guys we suspected of smoking, plus a fifth guy who had been laughing a lot too, all hopped over the boards and went to their positions. Easton won the face-off, waited for someone to knock them down or poke check them or challenge them in some way, but found instead that our Spazzes were all bunched around the red line looking lost. So, Easton skated a perfect four-on-one across the blue line—one of our defensemen *did* get back—and after whipping three snap passes they put it past Zip's back easily.

"Well," the left wing said to our bench with a

forced laugh as he lined up, "what do you expect from the Spaz Line?"

"As much effort as we get from the first line," Dooby called back. Then, to me, he said, "Ernie didn't even try a poke check. That's the only hockey move he knows, so he usually tries it six times a shift."

Not this shift. Coach left them out there against the amazed Easton skaters until the offense caught on and scored two more quick goals. Now it was 6–3, and the Easton guys had recovered their competitive sense. By the time Coach hollered "Change!" we had ourselves a different hockey game. The Spazzes didn't get another shift. We barely hung on to win 6–4, and it would have been closer but for Zip, who, luckily, was hot. I bet they outshot us 14–4 in the third period. We play whole *games* when a team doesn't get 14 shots against us.

When we got back to the locker room the place was a mess, with clothing and old equipment strewn all over the place. Barry, still completely in his uniform, was bent over a hockey bag slinging everything he could find over his shoulders. A bag he had already finished with, apparently, was empty and crumpled next to him.

"Hey, jerko," said Ernie, pushing past some of us into the room, "that's my stuff."

"Well, Erno," said Dooby, "then if I were you I wouldn't climb inside my bag right now."

Ernie had strode on his skates over to where Barry was tossing a sneaker out of his bag. "What do you think you're doing?" was the best he could manage. By this time the rest of us were watching from around the doorway. It was obvious that Ernie had decided that, come to think of it, he really didn't want a piece of Barry. Only a pitiful fool would want a piece of Barry, especially when he was angry, as he plainly was now.

"May I ask what you're looking for?" said Ernie, in a mock-haughty voice, making a stab with his left hand at the other shoe, which he missed. It smacked against the far wall.

"A bong would do," said Barry. "In fact it would be preferable because it is so large and would be easiest to find. But"—he flung out a pair of boxer shorts with a Black Dog pattern—"I'll take a pipe, or even some rolling papers. Frankly, I'd just as soon not come across any actual dope, because then all kinds of nasty problems of confiscation and prosecution would arise. Shoot," he said, standing up, holding Ernie's bag, which was now empty, and giving it a shake before dropping it in a contemptible heap. He looked around. "Which one belongs to that so-called left wing?"

"All right, Barry," said the voice of the coach behind us. Barry looked over, shrugged, and walked back to his own spot by his own bag, where he dropped to the bench and began to unlace one of his skates.

We all parted for the coach, who told us in a low voice to go ahead and get out of our uniforms and into our street clothes. He took Dooby's stick and lifted the pair of Black Dog boxers on the blade and said, "Ernest, I believe these belong to you?"

Ernie walked over and snatched them without a word.

We all got dressed in silence. Not even Cody threw a tape ball, and Shinny restrained himself from informing us when the last time was that a hockey team had dressed in absolute silence. Dooby coughed once—he couldn't keep completely quiet if his life depended on it—but otherwise there was nothing but an eerie series of noises, tape being ripped off socks, the slip of sweaty clothes sliding off skin, grunts as tight skates were pulled, and finally a rather neat conclusion of long zips as bags were closed.

Coach must have been counting zips, because immediately after what turned out to be the last one he said, "Prince, give me a moment before you sing."

"I'm not certain I feel much like singing today," said Prince.

"No, you should sing," said the coach, "because most of us deserve a song—we won a play-off hockey game against a more talented opponent, and it wasn't easy."

"It was harder than it needed to be," said Zip.

"Aw, did you have to make a few saves?" said Ernie.

"Don't push it, Ernie," said Dooby. "He'd kill you for a nickel." Then Dooby dug in his pants pockets, came up with a nickel, and flipped it to Zip, who made a stick save on it, picked it up, and glared at Ernie.

"Cut the crap," said Coach.

"But you *said* we weren't going to have to play," said the left wing.

Coach gave him a tight-lipped look that would freeze hot coffee. The wing looked down. Coach said, "Are you or are you not members of this ice hockey team? As of this moment, that is."

"We are," said the wing.

"Have you not practiced just as hard as Cody and Boot and Woodsie and Barry at every practice for two years, except perhaps for the last two, but we'll forget them for now?"

"We have."

"Because you came to the sport so late while others were starting at four and five years old, or because you lack athletic skill in general, or both, have you nevertheless worked your pants off to learn how this game works and been ready—no, *eager*—for your shifts on the ice during games?"

"Yes."

"And have I, your coach, fully capable of recognizing a good player from a bad, paid you back for your effort with full respect, playing you in your regular shifts, game after game, even when it meant you were on the ice in situations that might have turned out better for the team as a whole if I had replaced you with players of higher skill?"

"Yes, yes, okay, you—"

"Shut up. And has anyone in this room complained about this situation? I will take responsibility for telling you, because it would have been to me that such complaints would have been made. The answer is—*No*. Not one of these 'better' players has complained about your presence on the ice, even during key situations. Do you know why they have not complained?"

"Because they're nuts?"

"Do not dare to joke with this. These people around you have not complained because they *respect* you. They see you working, doing the best you can do as hard as you can do it, practice after practice and game after game, and when a game-saving or game-winning situation comes up and your line takes the ice, they think, 'Well, those guys earned it as much as any of us did.' Do you understand this?"

He asked each of the suspect players in turn. They had to each answer "yes" very loudly before he would move on.

"I am leaving the door to my office open to-night," Coach said. "I am also leaving open the lower drawer on the left side, which is a double-deep drawer. When I arrive at seven tomorrow morning I want to open that drawer and find all paraphernalia. I do not want to find any of what in Vietnam we called 'contraband,' however. I do not want any contraband brought inside a hockey rink. I want it taken out back and thoroughly mixed with a large, fresh pile of Zamboni snow until it is broken down and unrecognizable and utterly unrecoverable. I guarantee that you will not be disturbed while you do this. Do you understand?"

He asked each of the players in turn, and they had to answer loudly in the affirmative.

Dooby raised his hand. The coach nodded at him.

"Coach," said Doobs, playing with his fingers and looking at them, "I was, like, wondering—tomorrow, if it's, like, a decent bong, could I, like, buy it?"

Everyone in the room except Barry and the coach laughed. When the laughter had petered out, Coach said, "Doober, you don't play in the first period of the next game. Woodsie, you take his shifts. Any more questions?"

No one had any more questions.

"I have one more thing to say," said the coach. "I imagine the people who let the rest of you down out there today are feeling pretty bad. I don't want them to show it by a bunch of apologizing and humiliating behavior. Barry, you conduct a vote as soon as I leave: Do they stay on this team, yes, or no? If you vote yes, then today is forgotten—*if* they go back to their hustle. If you vote no, they go, and no hard feelings; from their side, because today they broke the law and we aren't turning them in, from ours because we have made them pay the heaviest fine we can levy. Okay?"

He left. Barry, trying not to sound angry, asked the question. Zip voted to kick them off, but everyone else voted to keep them on the team.

"Dooby just wants that bong," said Zip. "He'll think of some way to get it."

"Just so I can sell it to your older brother," said Dooby. Zip's older brother is a well-known prissy-clean kid who is also a fabulous and very gentlemanly hockey player. Everyone laughed, including the six smokers.

Prince stood up on a bench. "I will sing now," he said. And in his amazing voice, he sang the Velvet Underground's "Heroin."

We all left in silence.

six

My mother, who was my "hockey sponsor" I suppose you could say, was very happy with the turnaround our team had made. On the telephone, she listened to my summary of our first-place finishes and our play-off prospects.

"Excellence will out," she said. It had outed with her—she was a total whiz as a consultant with various government and private agencies, and had written several books. Plus, she had just accepted a guest professorship at Harvard, for which she had to fly in and out of Boston once a week, and so led a life of plane-cab-classroom-cab-plane. When I asked her if maybe she was taking on too much, she laughed and said her type did not admit that days could be filled. "Time is infinite," she said. "This minute we are in right now will never actually come to an end."

"Then you ought to be able to learn the oud

and write a book about rock climbing and go see the Taj Mahal before we're through," I said.

"Time should be spent *usefully*," she said. "Speaking of which, how's your father?"

My father worked as a printer, on flexible hours that let him raise my older sister and me, as much as we needed raising. He had zero ambition, beyond making sure everyone around him was having a decent time and pursuing whatever he or she thought would make for happiness. Recently, just after I decided to take up hockey, which complicated his life considerably, my sister decided to take up the bass viol, which complicated it even more. The bass viol is larger than an elephant and makes more noise too, until it is tamed. My sister had recently tamed it enough so that she could sight-read classical exercises and play them with the bow, then put on jazz records and pluck along with her fingers. I much preferred the latter way of exploring her new passion. I think she did too. My father, typically, refused to give an opinion, but just found a way of cheerfully squinching the instrument into his Volvo and driving her to both her classical and jazz lessons twice a week, which, when you consider all of my hockey practices and games, took some squinching of time, too. My mother gave him a good deal of child-support money, so his printing didn't have to cover everything. She also rented the bass viol and bow (those bows cost a lot). As she put it, my father was the "feel-good" parent, and she paid the bills.

My dad came to all my games. As we drove home from the first play-off, I asked, "Did you ever smoke pot?"

"Yes," he said. One of my father's great features is that he will not lie to you, even when the truth makes him look bad. "I smoked dope very casually in college for two years. It was kind of a social thing—you got together in someone's room to listen to a new Dylan record or something, and the next thing you knew, someone was handing you a joint and you took a hit and passed it on."

"Yet you would certainly wish that *I* not smoke pot, right?"

He nodded. "Right." He shrugged. "You learn things on the way to becoming parents—sometimes you learn you took chances you needn't have taken, and were lucky, and you hope your kids won't even take those chances because they might not get as lucky. Also—"

"What?" I asked.

"Well, I have read that because my generation made smoking dope so popular, so nearly *universal*, if you will, organized crime decided to step in and get a large piece of the action." He took a right-hand turn; I saw his mouth was as close to grim now as his mouth got. "I've read—and from enough sources that I believe it, by the way—that the production of marijuana is now a very slick commercial enterprise. Hell, when I was in college it was just a single-stem plant you grew in a clay pot on your windowsill! Now it's big business, and with the competition for that business, producers have used agronomical breeding techniques to produce stuff the potency of which makes my simple little kind of dope seem like drinking a Coke."

"There's stuff I've heard of called 'one-hit' dope," I said.

"Right. One hit and that's all you need to stay stoned for an evening. But don't you begin to wonder what happens if you take *two* hits? I think there's other stuff they add to the leaves now, too."

"I've heard cow tranquilizers are popular. The kind they give the cow before they kill it."

He nodded. "Would you—or your friends—really pick up and swallow some of the stuff they give cows before they kill them, if somebody put some on a table before you?"

"Of course not!"

He shrugged again. "I guess—and I haven't been passed a joint for thirty years, so keep my ignorance in mind—my guess is that when someone passes you a spliff at a party, that person doesn't give you a quick and chemically accurate rundown of what may have been sprayed on the marijuana in California when it was still in the whole-leaf form, before it passed through the fifteen steps it did to reach the plastic bag in your friend's jacket pocket. My guess is, that person has no idea."

"Right."

He sighed. "So I hate to sound like an old fogey, but—I'm not happy with even the possibility of you or your sister taking such junk into your bloodstream."

"Dad, this is turning into an anti-dope lecture.

But you really don't have to worry. I already decided not to smoke pot. Or drink."

"Then why did you ask?"

I shrugged. "Some kids on the team might have been smoking a little. But it's kind of been dealt with."

He nodded. "'Kind of?'"

"All right, it's been dealt with. Did you ever hear the song 'Heroin' by—"

"'He-e-e-ro-win, it's my life,'" he sang, poorly. "'He-e-e-ro-win, it's my wife.' Yeah, I've heard it."

"Prince sang it today. I don't think he learned that one from his grandfather."

"No, but I bet his grandfather has seen a few things in his time."

"That's what Prince says."

We were quiet for a while. Then my father said, "Were they the kids who had that awful shift in the third period?"

"That was them," I said.

"Don't worry—I won't say anything to anybody."

I waited a while, then I said, "The thing was, if Prince hadn't warned me a few days before, I wouldn't have *known*. Barry knew—he tore the kids' bags up, looking for pipes and stuff—and a lot of others just *knew*, but not me."

"And that bothers you."

"Well, yes"

He thought. "Why?"

I took a minute. "Because I don't always want to be a dumb-ass at parties and stuff."

"Some people go through life cool and much-liked, but they never get sophisticated, for some reason," he said. He smiled briefly. "I am one of them. I don't really know *poop*. But—" and he raised a finger—"that being said, it should be added that absolutely *anyone* can be cautious. For that, you need no special insight. You just have to always ask yourself, 'Can this hurt me?' Caution is a no-brainer: 'Can this hurt me?' It applies, oh, to telling lies, late hipchecks you're tempted to try, turning on the box in the bathroom while you're still standing in a pool of water, lots of things besides chemicals."

"I think I'm that," I said. "At least."

"I agree with you—you were born cautious."

"But I'm not sophisticated."

He shrugged, and sighed. "I guess you have to

decide—what's it worth to you?"

We finished the ride in silence, the kind of silence that is all right. As far as I was concerned, I thought my dad had said all he could. For someone who doesn't know poop.

seven

One practice per week was dedicated to a kind of intense personal skill the coach had never really focused on before, like making us skate at him across the blue line. He would poke-check the puck every time, until we learned enough about judging the backward speed and position of the defenseman's skates and the reach of his stick, and the proper way to curl our own blade over the puck a little to protect it.

Another time we spent ninety minutes learning to control the puck with our skate blades when our stick was tied up above our waist. He brought in these kids to help him each time, kids who played Midget A's or something, but kids who knew all the stuff he was trying to teach. They weren't as good at explaining as he was, but they were better at showing how to smooth these things into your game.

The other practice every week was ninety minutes of scrimmage. Before, scrimmages had always been pretty loose and offensive-oriented—there was a lot of scoring, a lot of flashy moves or attempted flashy moves, but not much hard hitting or checking.

Well, Coach said that was finished. From now on we were to scrimmage as if we were playing games—we learned to check hard, skate all out, and clobber each other, even little guys like Cody, and we started using the tricks we were learning. Scoring dropped way off: Prince's pretty passes got blocked by anticipatory skates, Boot got pushed out of position when he tried to set up at his corner of the net, Zip got screened, Dooby fired high slap shots from the point, Cody roofed it from in front. In one scrimmage, he hit Zip in the mask four times, and after the last one Zip skated out of the net over toward the coach.

"This hurts," he said.

"Go play softball," said Barry. "Right field would be good."

"Such a macho dude," said Zip. "Why don't *you* go ride bucking bulls or something? Hockey's about more than proving how much abuse you can take."

"You're both right," said the coach. "I've been running you pretty hard. This is a hard team now, Zip." He looked at Barry. "But hardness for the sake of hardness leads to mistakes."

"Like cross-checking your best center," said Zip to Barry.

Barry shrugged. "He got free and Cody had the puck for a centering pass."

"You could have lifted his stick or hipped him—he's a little guy and you're a big guy. Hey—you were supposedly protecting *me* and I thought it was too much."

"I didn't hear a whistle."

"Maybe you should have," said the coach. "Okay, Zip, I'll call the rough stuff tighter. But Barry—keep playing hard. Just keep your stick down. You could have pushed Prince in the back with a forearm and he would have gone down. You have to use your head to judge each situation—if you're trying to move a little guy, you can play differently than when you have to move a big guy like Shark."

"Yeah, so for *me* he can cross-check?" said Shark from down the ice.

"No, for *you* he can easily lift the stick, because despite your size you still haven't learned to use your arms to hold the blade on the ice firmly," Coach called to him. He looked at Barry. "Cross-checking Shark would be a waste. And you might get a penalty."

"I'll get some barbells," Shark yelled.

"Do," said the coach. "I'm serious. They might help. Just don't lift on game days."

Eventually Zip went back into the net and we resumed our scrimmage. I was embarrassed once when Coach stopped practice after I had snuck in to the top of the circle and gotten a snap past Zip.

"Stop it right there," Coach said. "Did everybody see how Woodsie shot?"

"Luckily," said Zip.

Barry, the last person you'd expect to be interested in shooting, except that he studies shots so he can stop them, said, "Instead of winding way up for a slapper, he pulled his stick about halfway back and got the shot off much faster."

"And what does that do to you as a defenseman?" said the coach.

"Well," said Barry, plainly uncomfortable with

having to talk so much, "slappers are really pretty easy to block, because the shooter's big windup gives you so much advance notice what he's going to do. But these little half-slappers can catch you by surprise. Plus I bet they're more accurate."

"Thank you," said the coach. "Nice shot, Woodsie. Face it off."

In a ninety-minute scrimmage my team scored only two goals and the other team scored only three. That's a far cry from the old days, when we probably got into the teens. I remember one scrimmage in which Cody had six goals all by himself. We were sore, too. We rarely got sore at our old practices, unless we skated lines.

It paid off in our next game, which was against a real clutch-and-hook team that used all the tricks we knew, plus some that were over the edge into plain dirty play, especially with their sticks. We were furious, and whenever we could we knocked the crap out of them. Our biggest hitter, Subtle, put two of them out of the game—not with injuries, mind you, just with rattled brainpans.

One of their forwards hooked Prince's gloves

up high once too often from behind—he had been doing it all day, as a way of catching up to the faster center—and the ref sent him to the box. On the power play Dooby saw a rebound rolling up the slot, skated by it and gave it a tap with his backhand. Then, on the ice, it made it through all the skates and sticks and miraculously went in under the goalie's pads. We won 1–0.

"Always put it on goal and good things happen, lads," Dooby kept proclaiming in the locker room. This is probably the oldest hockey cliché in the book.

"Always put it on goal and bad things happen, too," said Prince.

"Like what?" said Dooby, with a frown.

"If it happens to be *you* who puts it on goal, we have to listen to your mess all night," said Prince.

"I think everyone would agree with me that in a low-scoring game, the goal-scorers are entitled to their little moments of celebration."

"Oh, are you a 'goal-scorer' now?"

Dooby grinned. "I was tonight," he said. "How many did *you* get, Princer?"

"Barry," I called out. "What should any defenseman who scores a goal do?"

"Hang his head in shame," he said, removing a shin pad.

"There you go, Doobs."

The coach came in. "Nice shot, Doober," he said.

Dooby grinned around the room. "Thank you, Coach."

"And my apologies to the Spaz Line. I didn't give you a shift tonight because it was too tight."

"No problem," said Ernie. "We would have been out of our league out there."

The Spaz Line, by the way, had gone back to their hapless but hustling play during the week's practices, and I really think the incident of their playing stoned was forgiven and forgotten. I presumed the coach had received and disposed of their paraphernalia, while they smothered their contraband in Zamboni snow as prescribed.

"Who do we have next?" said Prince.

The coach looked at a paper in his hand. "York."

"Skate and shoot," said Prince. "We beat them twice."

"Don't get cocky," said Coach.

"Prince was *born* cocky," said Cody.

"*Hatched*," Dooby corrected.

"That's why I fly," said Prince, "while you're still lumbering around like a bear. Or a hippo."

"Whatever you are, be ready to practice Tuesday night," said the coach, and he left.

On Saturday we played York, and they were indeed a skate-and-shoot sort of team. However, they skated and shot a lot better than Easton. At one point late in the first period we actually found ourselves down 2–0.

"Don't panic," said the coach. "Let them skate, but force them wider—and let's have the center backcheck more to intercept centering passes. They'll wear themselves out by the third. And in our offensive zone, I want Woodsie and Billy to shoot more."

I got a goal almost immediately on one of those little half-slappers, and Billy scored from an impossible angle two shifts later—I swear he was straddling the goal line in the corner—and we got our claws into them as they started to wear out. Still, though, they scored once in the second on a bullet off a rush that Zip probably should have stopped, and the second period ended with them up, 3–2.

"Pound them," said the coach. "Hipchecks to pin the defensemen behind the net every chance you get, clean shots in the ribs in the corners, kick the puck around to keep it alive, and punish them for fighting for it. Make them skate, but nail them between the red line and their blue now, so they have to dump and chase. They're too tired to dump and chase, and all that corner stuff will wear them out completely."

"Why won't it wear *us* out?" asked Shark.

"Because *we've* been practicing it all month, chickenhead," said Dooby. "It's called 'conditioning.'"

It happened pretty much as the coach predicted. By the time their guys were taking their second shifts they were showing a little wobbliness; by their third shifts their speed was about two-thirds what it was in the first period, and their enthusiasm was about 20 percent. We tied it when Dooby pinned one of their forwards behind the net and I picked up the puck that trickled away from him, and just kept skating until somebody picked me up. But no one ever did, so I put the goalie down to the forehand side by dipping my shoulder as if I were going to shoot that way, then pulled it backhand and slid it in behind him. I made sure to hang my head in shame as I skated by Barry.

Prince, full of pep, skated in a sneaky circle around the defenseman who was supposed to watch him in the slot, so he was in front of the guy to get a nice poke-pass from Cody and fire it in. We had pulled ahead, and some of them lost their fight, though the rest tried hard to keep them excited. But it didn't work. We kept beating them up, frustrating their rushes wide, making them dump from the blue line, and they got tired and sloppy. Shinny scored untouched from the circle off a long rebound two of their guys had just watched slide past, and then Shark kept his stick on the ice long enough to deflect in a nice pass again from Shinny, and we won going away. They could barely shake hands afterwards and were too tired to say "Good game." We suddenly realized we were just as tired. It was a quiet but happy locker room.

Without us really noticing it, play-off victories were piling up behind us. Next Sunday we were to travel to New Jersey for some regional action. We had taken care of the area around us—a pretty large area, at that.

have become convinced that human beings can make themselves believe whatever they want to believe. It doesn't matter what the evidence is in front of a person's face—he can overlook it, or find an excuse for it, or blame it on somebody else. I'm sure this is not exactly an original thought. But everyone has to learn it for himself, and it hurts, so the resistance is strong.

At the second practice—the scrimmage—before we were supposed to go to regionals in New Jersey, Ernie played worse than he usually does. Now, even at the best of times Ernie is a terrible hockey player, with only one thing to recommend him: a rocket of a slap shot from the point, which may or may not end up on net, and, if it does end up on net, will almost certainly beat any goalie in our leagues and go in. Coach uses him occasionally on the power play.

Well, at this scrimmage Ernie kept stubbing his stick a few inches too far behind the puck when he shot, and thus kept hitting the puck on its top and sending it skittering away. For some reason the skittering pucks tended to go straight, and they went right at the net. Ernie would laugh a little too loud and say, "Put it on net and good things will happen—right, Doobs?" A couple of times good things *did* happen, when Prince or Shinny or Nathan would turn his shot into a pass and do something with it down low.

But for the games on Sunday, Ernie showed up bright as chrome and even got to play in the second game (we won both) and put one of his rocket shots in the top corner for a score. We were ahead by three at the time, so it wasn't a crucial goal, but hey, it was a goal, off a terrific shot.

But Tuesday at practice he was goofing around again, so much that the Midget A running the drill just kicked him out and made him go sit in the penalty box for about ten minutes. At scrimmage two nights later he was himself again; in fact he even hit Shark in the ear with one of his very wide shots, and Shark had to go to the hospital and get stitches—Ernie had cut him through his helmet.

We played two games Saturday in Philadelphia. We won the first 3–0 easily against a team from Delaware that had one good line and had ridden those three players this far into the play-offs, but we shut them down and they rode no further. The second game was against our old pals Hershey, probably the toughest team we played during the regular season *and* the play-offs because they play a lot like us—they're incredibly tight checking and hard hitting at every opportunity, and they have a few excellent and opportunistic offensive players who capitalized when they got the chance. You could not fall behind this team—even by a goal—because they could shut you down and come as close as hockey comes to stalling, firing it off the glass out of your offensive zone every time you tried to get something going.

We played well, but so did they; it was insanely tense, especially for us, because hundreds—if not thousands—of fans had come from surrounding areas of Pennsylvania to root for them. As for us, we had about twelve parents cheering us on. Because it was so tense, I don't think anybody noticed that down at the end of the bench Ernie was acting pretty loose—shouting silly things at Hershey players and the linesmen, and laughing way too much.

Early in the third a Hershey player made a rare mistake—he let Cody beat him to a puck in the neutral zone and had to haul him down very obviously. He got whistled for it, and we had a power play. Their coach called his timeout. Ours used the time to set our lineup: it was the first unit, but with a single change—instead of Barry at one defensive spot, Coach called on Ernie. He was going to unleash his secret cannon and hope he got lucky.

The face-off was in our zone to the left of Zip. Prince won it as clean as you could want and pulled the puck back between his legs to Ernie—a perfect set up. Ernie skated a few feet, setting up, and then laughed. It was unmistakable: Even then I thought it was tension, but it sounded so peculiar that everyone—even the fans—shut up.

Then Ernie unleashed his shot. Only this was one of his stubbers, which sent the puck skittering in toward the bloc of players set up in front of the goal. One of Hershey's penalty-killing forwards jumped on it and pushed it ahead, joined on the far side by another fast-thinking forward.

Dooby did the right thing. He turned, skated as fast as he could to their blue line, then swivelled and faced them skating backwards in front of Zip. If the other defenseman—Ernie—had just done the same, he would have made the rush a two-on-two, which confers no special advantage to the attacking team. But after stubbing his shot, Ernie stood frozen three feet inside the blue line, facing the direction in which he had struck his sorry shot, and as the puck carrier whizzed at him he made a lame attempt to fish for the puck with his stick. The puck carrier was by him in a flash, and instead of a two-on-two they had a two-on-one, and they worked it perfectly with two quick passes. Zip never had a chance. Suddenly, in the third period against Hershey, thanks to a witless goof by Ernie, we were facing almost certain defeat.

We were all pretty shocked at Ernie. I mean, we all knew him from last year before he had been a Spaz, and he had been at least capable of the fundamentals—he had never shown this kind of giggly incompetence before. I mean, he was acting as if he just didn't give a crap out there, but none of us wanted to believe that because we kind of liked him. Yet there was no doubt about his screwing up, and when he turned to the coach with red eyes and a very out-of-place smile that said, "Jeez, sorry, but what's the big deal? I'm just a Spaz anyway," I think we all felt a chill go through us. We knew something was wrong with Ernie, and I think we all knew what it was.

And so Hershey's players played their keep-away game with us for three or four shifts, getting possession, banging the puck through the neutral zone, and making us chase it down. They played carefully, took no chances, got well back on D, in fact kept a floater back in our offensive zone just so there could be no breakaways. The period—the game—ticked away. We were down inside two minutes.

But sometimes when things look blackest you just throw out your discipline and try something wacky. That's what Shinny did with a little more than 1:30 left. Carrying the puck through the neutral zone, with at least four defenders watching him *but not the goalie*, Shinny crossed the red line, wound up quickly, and let fly a zinger. The inattentive goalie reacted much too late—it went right under his blocker and into the net, a ninety-foot miracle goal, a cheapie, all because the goalie had so much faith in the defensive play of his mates. Shinny couldn't have hit the net seven times out of ten on the fly from that same spot, but it didn't matter—quirkier goals than that have won many Stanley Cups.

Prince and Cody and Boot took over from there. Naturally, the Hershey players were dejected. But there was a face-off to put the puck back on the ice, and the Hershey fans were stunned into a silence that hurt the players more than their wild enthusiasm had helped earlier. It was as if the players were going at half speed, and our first line—even the Boot—were juiced with pure electricity. Prince swiped the puck off a defenseman's stick, streaked toward the net until he had drawn two players, then circled tightly back to his right and snapped a pass to Boot trailing the play into the zone. Then the Boot one-timed it so rapidly you could not be sure he had even touched the puck. But there it was, in the net with the ref pointing at it, and less than a minute left on the clock.

Before the face-off Coach had put me in as an extra defenseman along with Dooby and Barry, and Prince pulled the face-off back to me. I skated back to the net behind Zip, waiting for them to come after me. When they did they left huge passing lanes open. I hit Dooby at the blue line and he popped it to Cody going full tilt across the red line into our zone. They had pulled the goalie, and Cody skated it up to the crease and waited until someone finally chased him almost down, before tucking it in. We won 3–1. I had passed the puck to Shinny before his miracle shot, and to Dooby before he hit Cody, so I led all scorers with two points. Needless to say, this was made the subject of much abuse in the locker room.

"A defenseman!" Zip rolled his eyes. "What do you say about *that*, Barry?"

Barry shook his head sadly. "He's out of the brotherhood."

With all the joking about my points, the condition and misplay of Ernie had been momentarily overlooked. But the sudden entrance of the coach, scowling, brought us all back to earth.

"Ernest Taylor!" called the coach.

"Yes, sir," answered Ernie, with much less humility than we expected.

"You are dismissed from this team. Turn in your uniform to me, minus the socks, before you leave tonight."

Ernie just stood there, in his long johns, suspenders, and hockey pants, staring back at the coach.

"May I know the reasons for this cursory dismissal, sir?" he finally asked.

"Don't give me that crap!" bellowed the coach, turning scarlet. "You were stoned out of your mind out there and you nearly cost us the game!"

Ernie looked the coach calmly in the eye, cast a glance around the room, then resumed his cool stare at him. "I will admit that a poor shot and poor defensive play on my part led directly to Hershey's goal, Coach. I sucked. But, as you know very well, sometimes I do that." He looked around the room, then back at the coach. "As for the charge that I was 'stoned out of my mind' it isn't true."

We must have all gasped at once. The coach was the first to recover his voice, "You mean to tell me you will stand there and deny—"

"I do," said Ernie. "And if you want to go on *claiming* it, I'd advise you to *prove* it first."

With that he took off his suspenders and went to work on his hockey pants.

We all looked around at each other. Ernie had obviously been wasted during that shift. But the idea that he would *deny* it had never crossed our minds.

Nor the coach's, apparently. He stood there with his fists clenching and unclenching, then he left.

Ernie wasn't finished. "And the same goes for all of you," he said.

"Oh, I don't think you need to worry about *us*," said Zip. He looked up and around and said loudly, "Is there anyone, *anyone* in this room who feels he or she has *ever*, at *any* time, had his good character defamed by the coach? And that includes you, Cody, you weeny poo-poo-head. Anyone?"

We all shouted "*No!*" and "*Never!*"

"Your problem's elsewhere, dude," said Zip coldly. "At least until we catch you."

"See?" shouted Ernie. "That sort of thing is actionable! This is no small matter!"

Barry stood up and slowly turned toward Ernie. "Neither am I," he said. "Once I have *proof*."

"If we plant a little something," said Dooby, "does that count as proof with you, big fellah?"

"I would think so," said Barry.

"I saw Barry bite a guy's arm off once, at the shoulder," said Dooby. We all looked at him. "I lie a *lot*," he said.

Apparently the idea of us planting something had Ernie in a tizzy, until Zip said, "Don't sweat it, Ernie. If we can't get a dumb clod like you fair and square, we don't deserve to be an Academic All-America Team that goes this far in the play-offs."

"Well," said Ernie, "I still feel a lot of hostility—"

"*Good,*" said Zip. "Mess up any more of our games the way you did today and, dope or no dope, we'll rip your duodenum out." He looked around. "Of course, first we'd have to explore a little to *find* the cussed thing."

"It's in the neck," said Cody.

"It's deep in the gastrointestinal cavity," I said.

"And, see, I've always heard it sits right there between the two lungs," said Zip. "So there's a lot of options, get me?"

"I doubt that Ernie will be seeing much ice time, anyway," I added.

Ernie wisely chose not to keep it going with more protests. But his eloquent and heated denial shocked us, and his use of all these quasi-legalistic words made us feel we were watching an alien instead of ol' Ernie. But the biggest thing that happened was that we all hardened toward him. He had suddenly worn out the last shreds of goodwill we felt toward him. Now we saw him as a dangerous stranger.

I finally left with Prince. "What do you think?" he said.

"I think we have to catch him at it," I said.

He nodded. "So we can chuck him and get on with it."

"Exactly."

He thought for a minute. "Can you come over later? After ten?"

"You got it."

nine

I trotted across wet lawns and through backyards, amazed at how many houses had closed down for the night by this hour, which was when I was usually just starting my last subject for homework or trying to talk my dad into letting me watch the last ten minutes of a Caps game on TV. I guess we're a late family, though we *do* always have the lights out by eleven.

At Prince's house there was only one light on, the room I knew was his, on the second floor. But as I cut through the backyard wondering how I was going to get his attention down here, his back door opened and a voice whispered, "A cracker running around wild at night just *begging* for a butt full of buckshot in *this* part of town." This is a joke, because the town we live in is mostly white, and this particular upscale housing development is *entirely* white except for Prince and his grandfather. I cut for the door, which Prince held open while I took off my wet shoes. In his house you always have to take your shoes off. It's one of his grandfather's crazy rules.

We went up the stairs quietly, down the hall to his room, and then inside. He closed the door. On his desk he had laid out a large piece of paper. I went over and looked. On one side he had written in the day of the week and the date of every practice and game we had run through since that first practice when I had noticed the four Spazzes laughing so much; apparently Prince had noticed too, though it wasn't until the next time that he had spoken to me.

He motioned me to sit at the desk, and I picked up his pen. Starting at that first practice, a few inches away on the paper, I wrote "Yes" or "No" for the first few occasions.

"Why not *'stoned'* or *'straight'*?" he asked.

"In case your grandfather sees this," I said with a shrug. "Somehow I can't stand the idea of him reading the word *'stoned'* like that. *'Yes'* could mean anything."

Prince nodded and put his hand on my shoulder, where he left it until I was through, all the way down to the Hershey game. Then I dropped the pen and we both studied the page. It was obvious.

"No pattern at all," he said.

"I wouldn't expect one, really," I said. "Dope smokers aren't like crack addicts. They can take it or leave it as it strikes their fancy."

"We ought to make a third column," he said.

"Of what?"

"Of who it was got stoned with him and when he did it alone."

"Good idea." So I wrote it out. It was obvious Ernie was the only one of the four—maybe five—who had kept up after the coach's lecture and the team's vote.

Prince rubbed his hands now. "All right," he said. "We now have ourselves what they call 'a human factor.'"

"The other guys?"

He nodded. "Think we can turn them?"

I thought about it. "Only if we convince them the team will throw them off too, along with Ernie.

The fact that they stopped shows they're more scared than he is."

"Or maybe they're just less stupid," said Prince.

"Ernie was about as stupid as you can get," I said. "That was *bound* to be the tensest game of the year, and he shows up whacked."

After a second, Prince and I looked at each other. "Tensest game. Whacked," he repeated.

"Looks like we got our proof," I said.

"He gets jumpy from the pressure of competition, *good* competition," said Prince. "When he knows in advance it's going to be tough."

I watched him think, and did some thinking myself. "Maybe we can plant some jumpiness—"

"—and lay a trap," he said. "I'm hip. Scare the poor dude, then snatch him while we know he's trying to soothe those nerves. But who's going to throw the scare? We don't know the teams, and he won't listen to us anyway."

"The coach," I said. We'll have to get the coach to build up one of the games as if it's going to be a real tight one so Ernie will feel enough pressure. Then we can catch him at it."

"You like that idea better than trying to turn one of the other guys against him?"

"*You* want to take a player who's cleaned up and make him a rat?"

He thought about it and shook his head.

"Okay, who talks to the coach, then?"

"I will," he said. He looked at me. "Seniority."

"You just want to suck up."

"I don't *need* to suck up. I'm already the center on the first line, you tanglefooted excuse for a defenseman. If anybody would look like a suck-up, it's you."

"Okay," I said. "When will you talk to him?"

He thought. "We have practice tomorrow night. I guess I can drop over in the afternoon."

"What if Cody wants to listen in?"

"Cody's completely cool."

"Should we let anybody else know?"

He shook his head. I started to speak, then he said, "Wait. I know. There's one small problem we haven't talked about. *How* to catch him. Two, maybe three of us can't cover much territory."

"Do we agree he's probably getting high close

to the rink? Close to the start of the game?"

He nodded, and thought. "Maybe we *could* ask one of the other three *where* they smoked. Maybe that isn't asking someone to become a rat."

I shook my head. After a moment he shook his, too. "You're right," he said.

"We need the team," I said. "I *do* know Saturday's games are at home, at our rink, which should make things a lot easier."

"Right before a play-off game we're asking everyone to become a dope detective," he said, shaking his head. "Great for the concentration. We'll be lucky to escape from the first period of that next game down no more than two goals."

"You might be surprised," I said. "I think getting this resolved might have the reverse effect—I think it's breaking up everybody's concentration *now*, only we aren't talking about it to each other, which is even worse than having a detective project involving the whole troop."

"What about the other smokers?" said Prince. "The ones who have stopped?"

I thought for a moment. "We can call them and

tell them but not ask them to help. We can tell them to just stay out of the way."

He thought. "Good. Now, I think it's better if we ask Coach to build up the second game of the day if he can. Because then we've got everyone hanging around the rink anyway, and if Ernie's going to smoke somewhere, it's likely to be close."

"And the lazy bozos will all just be playing video games anyway," I said, "so asking them to do a little something won't be like pulling them away from a careful player-by-player study of the opponent's roster."

He laughed. "The only player on the team who'd do *that* is *you*."

"Thank you very much. Now listen, what we have to do right now is divide up the rink into areas to be covered, and assign them to different players."

He thought. "This is getting pretty complex, isn't it?"

"No. It's getting organized."

"Typical white boy comment. All right. But one thing."

"What's that?"

"We have to make it clear to each guy we talk to that all we want to do is *catch* the dude. We don't want to overreact and tear his lungs out on the spot and cause a big scene. That *would* destroy any concentration we had on the game, as well as probably draw in adults, club officials, maybe even the law," Prince said. "And who knows? Maybe we'd have to go back and forfeit any games he played in, and that would be finito for us in the play-offs. We got to keep it *cool*, keep it a *team* thing, make Ernie feel he's simply being dismissed from the Wings, nothing more will happen to him despite Zip's big talk and Barry's strutting. He's *safe*—he can even go on smoking if he wants until the law *does* catch up with him. The *team* thing is, we *got* him, he's *gone*—let's go play hockey."

"Excellent," I said. "You tell Zip."

"Only if you handle Barry."

"Okay. Now let's make a map of the rink and divvy it all up."

* * *

It took us almost three hours. We kept remembering little nooks, inside or outside, where someone could hide for a quick joint, and we really had to stretch out the eleven players we had to work with. At several points each of us threw down the pen and said, "It's impossible," but always the other was hot to keep on going. In the end, we had a pretty decent looking map that Prince said he would roll up and show the coach tomorrow.

"And I guarantee," he said, "he'll make the opponents for that second game sound like the Red Wings."

"Let's just hope they're *not*," I added.

He laughed, and we shook hands, and he walked me back down to the back door. "Leave your shoes," he said. "We sell them to buy bread."

"I know better," I said. "I've heard your grandfather putting down the bread in this country."

Prince snapped his fingers. "Crap," he said. "I'll have to make it 'porridge' next time. Wouldn't a poor slave family want for porridge?"

"Just say you need to get your skates sharpened," I said. "If it's a member of the team, he'll gladly leave you the shoes."

He laughed, but the moon was so bright I could see him blush too. "'Bye," he said.

"'Bye. We'll catch this mother."

"We will."

I made my way back across the lawns. By now, all the houses were dark. I didn't even *want* to know what time it might be.

don't know about Prince, but I decided to make my phone calls at breakfast time. Almost all the guys on the team went to the same school, and I knew that school's schedule, and I got lucky with the other few. Only Dooby seemed cranky about being called so early, but he settled down right away when he heard what I had to say. So did everyone else. I got every person on my list, and they all agreed and seemed to understand where they were supposed to patrol on the sly. Billy wanted to wear black lines under his eyes, but I assured him it wasn't necessary. Barry was no problem about the no violence. Barry is really a very smart guy.

I passed Prince in the hall between third and fourth periods and all he said was, "A hundred percent. You too?"

"A hundred percent."

We didn't talk again in school. I did have two

classes with Ernie, but we just ignored each other. That was no problem. We usually did anyhow. He wasn't a buddy of mine.

I waited at home in the study by the telephone. I imagined Prince, trying to get free to make the call to me. "Is it a girl?" his grandfather would ask in French. Prince would probably tell him it was some serious hockey business that did *not* involve on-ice technique, a subject on which his grandfather feels he is an expert. If his grandfather thought the phone call I was waiting for had to do with planting your skate edges while holding a defenseman on your back or angling the stick blade for a backhand pass that went forward at an angle of more than 15 degrees, he would probably send Prince from the room and make it himself. Otherwise, he respected Prince's privacy.

At about six the phone rang. It was Prince.

"All set," he said.

"Who do we play?"

"A team from eastern Ohio. Coach didn't know much about them, but he had their record there, and they tend to win games by scoring six, seven, sometimes eight goals. The best sign is they played Hershey once in a Christmas tournament, and Hershey won 2–0. So they seem, shall we say, vulnerable to our style of play. Not as worrisome as if they had won all their games 2–1, like us. Coach says he can make them sound incredibly danger-ous—he invented a kid who is just coming back from an injury, who will increase their firepower no matter what kind of defense we try. Also, he's going to pretend that this is probably the hardest-skating team we will play, so because of sheer fatigue to our players he may have to go deep into our bench."

"That's pure genius! If *that* doesn't make Ernie nervous, nothing will. Do we need to call the guys again and tell them it's all not true?"

"I don't think so. Do you?"

"No. My only worry is that Billy will show up for practice tonight dressed as a ninja."

"Yeah, we need to keep a tight lid on Billy. Zip was fine, by the way. How was Barry?"

"Completely cool. What did Zip say?"

"'If I can catch pucks going eighty miles an hour through a screen, you guys ought to be able to catch one pot smoker in Vans.'"

"That reminds me," I said. "We should have a

few of our guys carrying skateboards, in case Ernie has one and tries for a quick getaway."

"It will hardly matter at that point. But okay, good thinking. Anything else?"

"Yes. I went to the grocery store and bought a few of those disposable cameras with a flash. Even if the pictures don't come out, making him *think* we photographed him in the act will throw a scare into him and maybe shut him up about 'actionable' crap and all that."

"Excellent. We'll hand them out when we meet in the Boys' room between games," Prince said.

Our rink has six bathrooms labeled Men's and one labeled Boys', and no hockey player older than seven would *ever* go in that room. It was as safe as any place against an intrusion by Ernie, unless it happened to be where he did his smoking. In which case, if he came sneaking in with his stuff during our meeting, he would save us all a lot of trouble.

That is a week for which I cannot recall any details of practice, except to say that Ernie seemed straight and hustled enough to be respectable, and that after our Thursday practice Coach gave a speech about our second-game opponents on Saturday that had *me* scared. If Prince and I had been as smart as we thought and Ernie smoked pot as relief from tension, then this would do the trick.

Saturday came. And first, of course, we had to win the earlier of the day's two games. In our arrogance, Prince and I had been assuming we would do this without any trouble. Well, we had all the trouble we could want. This was a team from North Carolina—a place difficult to associate with decent ice hockey—but they could play, and they knew it, and they had a little something extra to prove about their home state and probably the entire South. We kept lining them up for hits and somehow they kept slithering out of the major part of the impact; we kept poking at the puck as they flew in solo across the blue line, and they kept swerving at just the right moment and almost getting around us for short breakaways. They were well coached, but I noticed one flaw, or at least what I would call a flaw: On the power play (and they got plenty in the first period, as we kept having to haul them down from behind), their coach liked his defensemen to creep in so far that a pass across the top between them was dangerous, in that it ran the risk of getting poked and picked off by one of the penalty killers at the top of our box. Then, if he had any speed, he would have a clean breakaway all the way down the ice, because their defensemen would be left behind, still waiting.

Well, I quietly told our other penalty killers about this, and they were on the alert. But as it happens, the next time they were on the power play I was out killing the penalty, and at the top of the box too, and their right defenseman whipped the dangerous pass and I jumped at it and just poked it straight ahead with the blade of my stick, getting good wood on it. Then I just skated as hard as I could, catching up with the puck and pushing it ahead again and again, waiting for some hook from behind or some purple-shirted body to cut into my peripheral vision, but no hooks came and no speeding body cut in and the next thing you knew it was just me and the goalie. I honestly don't know what I did—this is unusual, for I don't have a lot of scoring moves and tend to remember them in great detail—but I do know that as I curved to the left to keep from running into the back boards I saw the puck dropping from high in the back string to the ice, well past the purple sprawl in front of it.

As so often happens, while the other team is psychologically recovering from a goal (in this case, a humiliating one because it was shorthanded), we jumped all over them and scored another, this one by Boot on a nice backhand off a Cody rebound that should have been cleared by one of the dudes involved in that pass I had intercepted. This goal was shorthanded, too—by about three seconds—and then we heard their coach lose it. He yelled at the players until the end of the first period one shift later, he yelled at them all the way through the period break, he kept yelling as their top line came out to take the face-off to start the second period. It was crazy. He completely demoralized his players. Maybe *he* was the one who thought he had something to prove about the South. Anyway, the team got a little hangdog, and we ate them up. Nathan actually got her first hat trick, and Cody had two. We beat them 7–0.

In the handshake line afterwards I said to one

kid whose moves I had really liked, "Hey—you got to get that coach to shut up, or you got to find a way to ignore him."

"He's the only person in three states knows enough to coach hockey," he said, "or so he tells us."

"He's not *coaching* hockey," I said over my shoulder as we passed on, "he's *yelling* hockey."

But when he shook my hand at the end of the line the coach also mussed my hair and said in a soft drawl, "Great anticipation, kid. Your opportunity was *my* fault, but the goal was all yours."

In the locker room we made a few jokes—mostly people inventing incredible shots once I confessed I had no idea what I'd done—but we tried to keep the atmosphere a good deal more tense than usual. Coach helped, by coming in just when everyone was almost finished dressing and saying, "Anyone need his skates sharpened? If so, get them sharpened *now*. I can't afford any dull edges this afternoon against *this* team. And first line? Forget the fancy passes—this coach and these players are too smart to let anyone get open long enough to receive one of Prince's Montreal-pastry specials. What else? No more than two pieces of pizza between games, and *nothing* to eat for an hour before face-off. Clear?" He left.

We all acted like we were shaking in our socks. I stole a glance at Ernie. Maybe it was my imagination, but he looked *extra* pale.

Prince didn't even sing.

eleven

We all gathered in the Boys' room as planned. It was empty. Billy was not wearing black stripes beneath his eyes. The other guys were silent while Prince and I went over assigned areas for patrol. A few raised their eyebrows when I handed out the cameras.

Then Zip spoke. "You know, this sucks."

"Yeah," said Dooby. "Going after one of our own guys feels like cat pee-pee."

"We're not going to line him up against the wall and shoot him," Prince reminded them.

"Still," said Zip.

"Would you rather go through the rest of the play-offs worrying about whether or not we have a stoned player on our bench? A player who may talk another player or two into smoking before big games?" said Barry, almost bitterly. "I say let's get this *over* with. I actually feel sorry for the guy too, he doesn't think he's doing anything so bad, but what he's doing sure doesn't go with play-off hockey, and *that* is all we're taking care of for now."

I looked at my watch. I had been assigned the job of 'floater,' kind of wandering from place to place to check on our coverage of the rink, maybe to come up just after one of our guys had passed, in case Ernie figured out what we were doing and timed his smoke by the passing of his 'sentry.' "It's time," I said.

"Let's get it," said Prince, and made for the door. Everyone shuffled out behind him.

And I came last. Floating.

We had ninety minutes until face-off. We figured for a high to last through an entire game, the guy would try to get in his smoke as close to changing time as possible, and that was only about forty-five minutes away. It was pretty dark outside, and I decided, after a quick run through the building, that outside was where we would find him. So I pushed out into the night, which was windy and cloudy and darker than the three-quarters moon would usually make it.

I must say, we made a pretty subtle bunch. Even

though I knew where everyone was supposed to be patrolling, I had trouble finding four or five guys who were really using the shadows of the building and its angles very well. I went from the doors in the middle to one corner, then turned and came back past the doors to the other corner. Both sides and the back were completely flat brick walls offering no secret nooks, so with the exception of one guy posted inside the sliding door at the rear where the Zamboni went out to dump and came back in, we hadn't wasted anyone on those walls. The guy nearest the corners was responsible for casting a quick look along the sides now and then, but we really couldn't see Ernie choosing them as his hideaways.

I did the passage along the whole front of the building and the parking lot twice more, and got negative reports whispered to me at every post. Time was getting on. I made another run through the building inside—nothing, and all the locked doors made checking pretty easy—and then another two passages along the front, getting more and more anxious. Something in me *knew* Ernie was out here, but we were coming up with nothing.

During my last pass Prince scooted out of a

shadow and pulled me into another.

"He's here, Prince, I *know* it," I said.

"You got that right," he said, and inhaled deeply. "Smell that?"

I took a deep breath from the bluster swirling around our nook. And there it was, unmistakable to anyone who has ever strayed into the wrong room at a party—the niff of marijuana burning.

"Great!" I said. "We can follow the smell backwards and we—"

Prince was shaking his head. "Tried it. This wind is too confused. Blowing this way, then that— all we know is he's out here somewhere."

I cursed, and looked at my watch. In about ten minutes, we would be expected to head for the locker rooms.

"I even checked out back with Shinny," said Prince, "to see if maybe it was stronger, or was collecting in the Zamboni door—"

"Wait!" I said. "I think I got it!" I thought back for a few seconds, and remembered the coach, that first time, instructing Ernie and his fellow smokers to destroy their 'contraband'—by going out. Away from the rink, to the place where the Zamboni dumped its snow. And he was also *guaranteeing* that no one would disturb them—meaning he had squared it with Marsh, the Zamboni driver, to look the other way.

"Do you know where Marsh dumps his snow?" I said.

Prince did the arithmetic and said, "Let's go."

We tore along the side of the building, ignored Shinny's wave from the closed sliding doorway, and ran hard and low down a narrow road that angled away from the rink into the darkness. The marijuana smell got stronger.

"There's two bigger old piles of snow at the corners of the road where Marsh dumps when it's raining," Prince whispered at a pant. "Beyond it there's a small paved lot with about fifteen piles a couple of feet high. Nothing to hide behind, but we got to take the corner piles and peek."

Then they were right there, about four feet tall each, and we dove into the snow on the rink side of them. But before we dove, I had just caught sight of a figure standing smack in the middle of the lot, with its back to us, and around its head an orange penumbra of light.

Prince looked across, and made his fingers walk, asking if I wanted to try to tiptoe closer. I nodded, my chest pounding so hard I couldn't believe Ernie was unable to hear it.

We stood up. There was another orange penumbra, and a gasp, then, as we took slow steps closer, the sound of an exhalation followed by four deep gasps that made the orange light shine like a searchlight that had just nailed its man.

Prince and I both leaped to the side of the figure, bringing us even with him. He looked my way, with his lips tight, his cheeks distended, his eyebrows raised, just as my flash went off. He kindly turned his face at Prince in time for Prince to get a good portrait, too. It was Ernie, and between the index finger and thumb of his right hand he held about two inches of an irregularly shaped cigarette.

"Proof enough," I said.

"You off the team, baby," said Prince, in his best street patois.

Ernie flicked the joint away toward a bank of snow and had the bad luck to hit it, so the ash went out with a hiss and we had a little more evidence, if we needed it. Then an explosion of smelly smoke came from his mouth. Ernie did not turn and try to run. I think we were a little surprised—we had become so used to Ernie the Killer Alien that we had completely forgotten that this was a thirteen-year-old kid we were nabbing, and furthermore, one who we had known as a pretty decent guy before he started with the smoke and whatever else there was.

Instead of running, Ernie just stood there and started to cry.

Prince and I looked at each other. In our Super Combat mode we had not been ready for this. We were more prepared to cut off routes of escape and holler "Pursue thirty degrees west!" and stuff like that. We were not prepared for a kid who used to be our friend simply crying.

"I get so nervous," Ernie sobbed out. "I know I'm just a Spaz and everything, and you guys and Coach are really nice about all that, but I can't help it—even as a Spaz I get scared to death."

"Well, in my opinion, which I offer as an extra benefit," said Prince, not too harshly, "you're looking in the wrong box to find your nerve. You find your nerve by looking for your nerve. But in any case—we got you, man. You broke the deal."

Ernie nodded, trying to stop his blubbering.

"Listen. Ernie, you think you could keep it if you had one more, secret chance? Just from Prince and me." Ernie turned his red face to me, but I was looking at Prince and he gave me a small nod.

"A chance? But the deal—" Ernie began.

"The deal is, right now nobody knows you were smoking dope again but Prince and me. And maybe we're willing to let you skip tonight's game. We can come with some excuse that won't make it sound like you were just being a jerk. You can pick up your bag and hightail it across this field without anybody else knowing, and you get your 'one more chance' back. But listen—you have to tell us the truth: will you do it, stay clean I mean, through the play-offs?"

"You guys—" Ernie gave us this sort of pathetic grateful look.

"Forget the gratitude," said Prince. "Hurry up."

"I'll do it," said Ernie.

Prince had already slung Ernie's bag from beside a snow pile, and it landed heavily at Ernie's feet. "Then get out of here," he said. "And one thing—

if you *do* screw up, and get caught, and kicked off the team, we never had this conversation. Swear, even as a bad guy?"

"Swear." Ernie wasted no time. He picked up his bag and vanished into the night. Prince and I trotted down the road and told everyone we hadn't found anything. We never said a word to each other about it. The team gave up and went in to change for the game.

twelve

The coach, who must have found out our detective work failed, came in once briefly just to warn us not to treat the game as an anti-climax. Cody asked what an anti-climax was. Coach left, shaking his head.

I know at least Prince and I were watching Ernie pretty closely during the following week's practices, and he did nothing wrong. Because of his big denial-threat deal, he wasn't exactly popular anymore. He hustled, unsmiling, and seemed to be playing the way you'd expect Ernie to play before this whole mess started.

The test came Sunday. Coach had told us at our last practice that the team we would be playing in the morning was a very tough one from Northern Virginia, and he expected a tight, scary game. Prince and I had no time to keep an eye on Ernie; we had our hands full of Northern Virginia. They checked us tight, we checked them tight, but then early in the third period one of their defensemen fell down swiveling to skate backwards—tough break, but that's how it can go—giving Reed and Nathan a two-on-one, and Reed buried it for the first goal of the game.

As we so often do, we pounced while they were still demoralized, and Reed got in one-on-one against a defenseman and just undressed him with some unreal moves, then burned the goalie with a roof shot that knocked his water bottle twenty feet into the air. Four shifts later Prince fired it in through the five-hole when everyone expected him to be thinking "Pass!" and we suddenly had a 3–0 lead with one minute left.

The coach called down the bench, "Spaz Line!"

With big whoops the usual guys clambered over the boards and lined up for the face-off. For the first time Prince and I got a look at Ernie.

Our hearts dropped.

Ernie was wasted. The first time the puck came to him, he tried to pass it across to the other defenseman, but he did it much too slowly. Their center intercepted and took it in on Zip all alone. It so happens he was a pretty spazzy center himself—

the other coach was giving his reserves some ice time too—and Zip poke-checked him easy. But as Ernie arrived to clear the long rebound he just looked down at the puck, his stick six inches off the ice, and it went to one of their wingers who wound up for a full slapper, unchecked by Ernie, and fortunately rang it off the post. Zip eventually smothered it for a face-off.

"Change!" called Coach angrily, even though there were only twenty seconds left.

But Ernie didn't skate back to the bench with the other Spazzes. And he didn't stick around for the postgame handshake lines. When the coach had hollered "Change!" Ernie headed straight for the gate, banged the glass to be let off the ice, and without looking back walked to the locker room. After we had finished it off 3–0 and shook hands and joked around a little, we all kind of tentatively entered the locker room ourselves. I think we half-expected it to be trashed.

But it wasn't. Far from it. It was empty. And there, in the spot where Ernie usually dressed, was his Wings sweater, folded neatly. His bag was gone, and so was he.

Nathan walked over and casually picked up the sweater, letting it tumble unfolded. "Yo, Coach," was all she said, and she tossed it high to the coach, who caught it without a word and went out. Prince and I snuck a look at each other, or thought we did.

"It was a decent try," a voice said quietly, and when we whipped our heads we found it was Zip who had spoken, seriously for once. He didn't even look at us, but was completely occupied with his buckles. How he found out I'll never know, but neither do I expect the word to go any further.

thirteen

The next game was a laugher.

On his first shift, the kid we call Subtle went into the corner full speed and completely clean, and put their *two* leading scorers on the bench for the rest of the period. We found out their goalie would flop down if you looked at him mean, and we kept flipping shots over his shoulders. By the time the second started we were up 4–0.

I honestly believe no hockey team can beat us when we play our way. I honestly believe no hockey team will, this year.

It got to 5–0, then a rebound hopped Dooby's stick and a kid knocked it in for 5–1. Midway through the third with that score holding, the coach called down the bench for the Spaz Line. A huge cheer went up, but only four players scrambled over the boards onto the ice.

"You're missing a Spaz defenseman now, Coach,"

Prince reminded him. "Got to demote somebody to take his place."

"What's this 'demote' crap?" hollered the Spaz center from the ice. "We consider it a *'pro*motion' to join the Spazzes, and this talk of *'de*mote' may very well be *actionable.*"

I hopped the boards. "I got it, Coach," I said, and skated to the left defense spot.

"Don't go hogging the puck with your coast-to-coast rushes," said the center over his shoulder.

"Don't worry," I said. "Wasn't so long ago I was a genuine Spaz myself. It'll come back naturally."

It didn't. But I played the role proudly.